To ⌐⌐⌐⌐⌐

All Love

Mommy Daddy

X o+o
X o+o

THE ORANGE PONY

Also by Wendy Douthwaite

THE CHRISTMAS PONY
A PONY AT MOOR END
A VERY SPECIAL PONY

THE ORANGE PONY

Chapter 1

"Oh, no! Not the Orange Pony!"

Kate felt the colour drain from her face as she spoke. Janet Delwood, the owner of Oakhouse Stables, looked at her in surprise.

"But, Kate," she said, reproachfully, "Tania's a lovely ride. I know she's a bit ... well ... *difficult* with other ponies, but I'm sure you'll manage." She smiled encouragingly at the eleven year old, who looked back at her with such wide-eyed horror. "You don't get much riding practice on old Darkie, you know," she continued. "We really keep him for our beginners – he's so slow and reliable. But you've been coming to Oakhouse Stables for four months now – it's time you moved on to a more *lively* mount."

"But I *like* riding Darkie."

"Well, I can't help it, Kate. Darkie's got a nasty cough and I don't want to send him out until the vet has seen him. You wouldn't want to risk making him ill, would you?"

"Of course not," Kate replied, hastily. She sensed a slight impatience in Janet's voice, and she was aware of Paula Holt watching her from outside Lancelot's stable, her eyes scornful.

1

"It's all right," Kate added quickly, "I'll ride her."

Janet looked relieved. "I'm sure you'll enjoy it," she said, turning back towards the tack room to answer the shrill call of the stable telephone.

Kate's spirits were low as she pushed her bicycle across the stable yard and propped it against the back wall of the tack room. Out of sight of the others, she fought back the tears which threatened. How could she explain to Janet – or to anyone – the fear that overtook her when she thought of riding the Orange Pony.

In fact, Kate thought miserably as she delved into her saddle bag in search of an apple for Darkie, how could she explain to anyone – or even to herself – how terrified she felt of riding *any* pony, except perhaps Darkie. She loved *ponies,* but riding them frightened her. Darkie was different, she thought fondly. Little Darkie was quite old. Janet was not sure, but she thought he was about twenty-two. Added to that, he had a very gentle disposition; and even Kate, who was his greatest fan, was bound to admit that he *was* a trifle lazy. To encourage Darkie to break into a trot was a tiring experience for his rider's legs, and to make him canter was practically unthinkable!

As Kate approached the stable block, the subject of her thoughts put his head over the end door. Two small black ears were pricked expectantly between a wild, unruly mop of mane, and a pair of

2

gentle brown eyes watched Kate's approach with interest. Below his soft black muzzle, Darkie's lower lip hung, trembling with anticipation.

No one could feel afraid of riding such a dear old thing; but the Orange Pony . . . Kate shuddered at the thought, as she rubbed Darkie between his ears before sliding back the bolt of the stable door. The apple was soon gone as Darkie munched happily, pushing his soft nose into Kate's hand in search of more.

"Don't worry," said Kate, "I've more for later on." She smoothed his neck and tickled his nose. "You're a greedy little pony, you know," she told him fondly. "Still, I mustn't tell you off," she continued. "You're not very well today, are you?"

As if he understood, Darkie put his head down and coughed.

"Oh, poor little Darkie," Kate murmured. "I hope you'll be all right."

The light from the doorway darkened, as Paula looked over the stable door.

"Time to get going," she called, and Kate was sure that there was a malicious gleam in her eye.

Kate let herself out of Darkie's stable, her stomach turning over and over in anticipation. Looking towards the group of ponies gathered at the far end of the stable yard, she wondered if she should simply go over to Janet and tell her that she could not go. Then she saw the watchful eyes of

Paula, who stood beside Lancelot, the big powerful grey which Paula liked to ride. Holding on to Lancelot's reins, she was in charge of Tania's reins, too, but she held the other pony at arm's length. The red ribbon was tied firmly in place at the top of Tania's tail, warning other riders that she might kick.

As she walked reluctantly towards the ponies, Kate found herself wondering why they all called Tania the Orange Pony. She was, in fact, a pale dun colour, with black mane and tail, black stockings and black-tipped ears – which now were flat against her head. Kate's stomach began to churn again as she saw Tania's expression; mean was the only way in which she could describe it.

"Could you take her away from the others?" Paula said. "She makes them nervous." Kate was surprised to see that Paula, too looked uncertain.

Plucking up her courage, Kate took hold of Tania's reins and tried to lead her away. Tania flattened her ears even more and looked at Kate sullenly.

"Come on, oh *please*, Tania, come on," Kate begged, tugging at the reins.

Janet came to her rescue. "Hold both reins firmly, close to her chin, Kate," she said. "That's it. Now, don't try to pull her; go round to the other side and push her head away from you and give her shoulder a little push." When Kate did as Janet suggested, Tania turned, and Kate was able to move her away from the other ponies.

"It's no good trying to compete in a tugging match with a pony," Janet advised, holding Tania's reins while Kate mounted. "The pony will always win because it's stronger. Now – how does she feel?"

"Not too bad," said Kate, doubtfully.

"Well, try and keep her away from the others." Janet looked at Tania thoughtfully. "It's a shame that she's the way she is with other ponies," she said. "I didn't realise when I bought her last September. She's so pretty in the summer – a lovely apricot, almost orange colour. She's very frightened of the other ponies, though, and that's why she kicks and bites."

"*Frightened* of them?" Kate echoed, looking surprised.

"Well, you know what they say," Janet laughed as she moved away to mount Charlie, her big dark bay cob, "attack is the best form of defence!"

Kate held Tania back while the rest of the ride moved off, and then squeezed her tentatively with her heels. Her heart was pounding as Tania moved away and began to walk behind the other ponies. Kate had seen Tania in action during other rides, when her rider had allowed her to come too close to another pony. Back would go Tania's ears and out would go her neck. Bared teeth would nip the hindquarters of the other pony, which would squeal with pain and annoyance. Sometimes

5

Tania's hindquarters would swing round as she aimed a kick at the unfortunate other pony. Then a ripple of disturbance would run through the group of ponies, and someone would shout, "Watch out – it's the Orange Pony again!"

And I'm riding her, Kate thought despairingly. I shan't be able to manage, I know I shan't. Her hands trembled. I'll make a fool of myself and Paula will give that horrible snigger. Kate saw Tania's ear flick back. She *knows* I'm frightened, Kate thought. That'll make her even worse.

Kate tried to quieten her trembling hands, and gingerly eased herself more comfortably into the saddle. She had to admit that the Orange Pony *did* have a nice swinging stride; it was very different from little Darkie's slow plod. But at least she was safe on Darkie. On the Orange Pony, she didn't know *what* might happen.

Up at the front, Janet raised her riding crop as a signal to trot. "Trot on!" she called, squeezing Charlie into a gentle trot. The other ponies followed, and Kate squeezed Tania into a trot, too. They were well behind the others, and Tania trotted out briskly, her ears pricked forward for once. It was a bouncy trot, but comfortable, and Kate was surprised to find she was almost enjoying herself. Soon, however, they caught up with the ambling pony at the back, and Tania slowed down, putting her ears back. Kate felt her stiffen.

"Steady, girl," she said, trying to sound reassuring, but her voice quavered.

Janet called a halt at the main road, and then they all crossed over. This was the part that Kate had dreaded. The ponies' hooves were thudding gently now, for they had turned off the road on to the Downs. They trotted sedately down the wide grassy path, and then Janet halted. All the ponies stopped, and Kate held Tania back.

"We'll have a little canter now, shall we?" Janet said. Kate's hands tightened on the reins. She might be all right if she could only keep Tania away from everyone else.

Janet turned Charlie round and pointed back the way they had come. "We'll canter back along the ride, and then we'll do some practice drill in the open," she said.

Trembling with fright, Kate turned Tania round and tried to keep her well away, but the pony sensed the approach of the others; her ears flattened against her head and her hindquarters stiffened.

"Come on, everyone!" It was Paula who shouted and kicked her pony into action. Pushing past, too close to Tania, she set off at a fast canter, shrieking at her pony, "Go on, Lancelot – go *on*!"

The other ponies surged past Tania, and the dun pony kicked out wildly. Kate lost one stirrup and, as she did so, Tania set off after the others.

Kate had never been so fast on a pony before. Terrified, she clung to the pommel of the saddle and fumbled with her foot until, at last, she found the lost stirrup. She moved her grip from the saddle to Tania's black mane, and then she gathered up the dropped reins. The ground sped past at an alarming rate.

"I'll never, *never* ride again," thought Kate, as she and Tania galloped on. They were catching up with the other ponies. Finding a gap, Tania galloped through, her ears flat against her head and her long black tail streaming out behind her. For a moment, Kate saw the amazed faces of the other riders, and then she and Tania were on their own, galloping down the long grassy ride.

Some of Kate's fear had left her, and she started to pull on the reins. Tania's pace began to ease. Kate pulled again, and at last they were cantering. Tania's ears were forward now, and Kate was amazed to find herself enjoying this ride; the smooth, steady stride of the dun pony; the gentle thudding of hooves; Tania's black mane brushing against her face.

Of course, it had to be Paula who spoiled it all. Kate saw Tania's ears flick back, and then press tight against her head. She turned to look, and as she did so Paula surged past on Lancelot. She was still shrieking and her arms and legs flapped wildly. But Lancelot was too close for comfort for Tania, who twisted sideways and let fly with her heels.

Kate felt herself slipping, and the next moment the ground hit her shoulder painfully. She felt herself tumbling over and over and then she was still. She struggled to a sitting position and became aware of two things – Tania, her head lowered, peering at her and snorting excitedly, and pain in her shoulder which made her feel sick if she tried to get up.

Hot tears forced their way down Kate's cheeks. She had known it would end like this – and it was all the fault of that horrible Orange Pony. Blinking through her tears, she saw Janet hurrying over, and behind her was Paula, astride Lancelot, looking at Kate scornfully.

Chapter 2

"No more riding, I'm afraid," said the doctor, peering at Kate over the top of his spectacles. "Not for a week or so, anyway, until that shoulder gets better. You're lucky not to have broken anything."

Kate gazed out of the window, as the doctor scribbled out a prescription. He needn't worry, she thought, I'm *never* going to ride again. I *hate* ponies.

Dad led the way out of the casualty department. When he had closed the door, he looked at Kate.

"How does it feel?" he asked, anxiously.

Kate noticed how strained his face looked. That's my fault, she thought. Dad, who was still recovering from a bad car accident nine months ago, was supposed to have as little worry as possible. Apart from extensive injury to one leg, he had received head injuries, and had been in a coma for a while. Miraculously, he had suffered no brain damage, but had been left with severe headaches which were sometimes brought on by worry.

Kate smiled back. "Don't worry, Dad," she said. "I feel fine." This was not strictly true, for her shoulder hurt every time she moved her arm, and every step jolted it painfully. After the X-rays, a nurse had fitted a sling under Kate's left arm, and this had helped, but Kate had been glad to accept some pain-killing tablets.

The pain had eased a little by the time they reached home. Mum was back from work, and had read the note that Dad had left. Having seen the two of them walking down the street, Dad leaning on his stick, and Kate holding her painful arm carefully in its sling, Mum opened the front door of the flat. Kate's spirits lifted when she saw Mum laughing. Mum wasn't the kind to panic or get into a state about anything, especially since Dad's accident.

"What a couple of crocks!" Mum chuckled. "You look as though you're both back from the wars!" Her glance took in Dad's tired face and Kate's pained eyes. "Come on in," she added gently, putting an arm around Kate's uninjured shoulder, "I've made a pot of tea. Come and tell me all about it."

The warmth and security of home enveloped Kate for the rest of the evening, and it was not until later on, when she was alone in her bedroom, that she thought about Oakhouse Stables and the ponies. She thought about Darkie and wondered what the vet had said about his cough. "But I'm not going back there again," she reminded herself. However, as she settled awkwardly in bed, trying to lie on her uninjured side, for some reason the sight of the Orange Pony's face looking down at her lingered in her mind. Why hadn't Tania cantered on, away from the other ponies, she wondered sleepily. Why had she stopped when Kate had fallen off? Kate drifted into an uncomfortable sleep.

When Kate awoke the next morning, she ached all over, and bruises had appeared all down her left side. Mum came in to see her. She gently pulled back Kate's pyjama top to view the painful shoulder.

"Goodness – you've got a massive bruise coming out on your back," she told Kate. "It'll feel a lot less painful once the bruising comes out," she added.

It was Sunday, and normally Kate would have been up early and off to the stables to help. Her weekly ride was on a Saturday morning, but she usually spent as much time as she could at the stables, mucking out, grooming the ponies and doing any other odd jobs that were needed. This morning, however, Kate wandered aimlessly around the small flat.

"I suppose I'd better finish my homework," she sighed at last, gazing mournfully out of the lounge window at the street outside.

Mum looked up from the Sunday newspapers. "Why don't you walk up to the stables?" she asked.

"It isn't very far, after all, and you can at least see your beloved Darkie."

Kate continued to stare out of the window. "I'm not going there again," she said bleakly. In actual fact, she longed to see the ponies, especially Darkie – and, although she could not understand why, the Orange Pony. But she could still hear Paula Holt's words . . .

When they had returned to the stables after Kate's fall, Kate had been standing outside the tack room, waiting while Janet backed the Land-Rover across the stable yard, so that she could take Kate home. Paula's strident voice had floated out from the tack room.

"But she's so *wet*," she had said contemptuously. "She's always so *timid* . . . and she *cried* when she fell off!"

"Well, I expect it *hurt*, stupid!" Clare's indignant voice floated out, too, as the Land-Rover pulled up beside Kate. Kate did not hear the rest of the conversation, but Paula's words remained in her mind.

Now, as she gazed gloomily out into the street, she thought, "Paula's right – I *am* wet. I can't get on a pony without shaking with fright, even though I love ponies. Oh, why am I so *stupid*?"

Miserably, Kate wandered back to her bedroom and sat at her desk, trying to set her mind to her history homework, but somehow the activities of King Henry VIII had lost their interest. Kate chewed on her pencil and glowered at the horsey posters on her bedroom wall.

Kate heard the telephone ringing and then, a little later, her bedroom door opened. She turned round, and Dad was standing in the doorway, looking at her thoughtfully.

"That was Janet," he said. "She wondered how you were feeling after yesterday. I told her you didn't feel up to going to the stables today. Janet said she missed your help."

Kate looked away from Dad's questioning gaze, and fiddled with the braiding on her chair as he continued, "She said troubles really *do* seem to come in threes," he said. "First Darkie's cough, then your fall — "

Kate looked up quickly. "What was the third?" she asked.

Dad stepped into the room and settled himself on the end of Kate's bed before beginning. "Well, apparently, when the girls went to fetch the ponies from the field this morning", he explained, "they found one of them with its front legs torn and bleeding. They don't know how it happened."

"Were the pony's legs badly cut?"

"Quite badly. Janet had to have the vet again. She said it could have been a lot worse, though."

"How do you mean?"

"Well, Janet seems to think that some barbed wire must have got wrapped around the pony's

15

legs – the vet thinks so, too. Janet can't understand how it freed itself. She said the pony could have done a lot more damage to itself if the wire had made it fall. It might have panicked and hurt itself really badly."

"Which pony was it?" Kate asked.

"Oh, I can't remember." Dad thought for a moment. "It began with T – Tiny, I think," he said.

Kate frowned slightly. "Tiny . . . no, there's no . . . Oh! Was it Tania?"

"Yes, that's it."

"Oh dear – poor Tania!"

"You know that one, do you?"

"She's the one I told you about; the one I fell off – the Orange Pony."

"But I thought you *hated* her." It was Dad's turn to look puzzled.

Kate bit her lip. "Well . . . I suppose I don't really hate her . . . " she said, slowly. "It's just — " She looked towards her father. "I'm so *frightened* of riding," she blurted out. "I love the ponies, but I'm so scared in case I fall off. Oh Dad, I feel so silly . . . so *feeble*. What can I do?" Tears of despair trickled down Kate's cheeks and she rubbed them away angrily. She hadn't wanted to say anything to her parents. They had been so pleased about deciding that they could afford to let her have riding lessons.

Kate had wanted to ride for as long as she could remember. She had gazed longingly at all the ponies and horses that she had ever seen – ponies from riding schools, beautiful, elegant police horses, cart horses. She had thought about ponies, drawn ponies, lived ponies – and now . . .

"Why am I so *stupid*, Dad?"

"You're not stupid at all," Dad replied quietly, handing her his handkerchief. "You just listen to me a moment."

Chapter 3

"Last year, when I had that accident," Dad began, "it was a very bad time for all of us. I didn't know anything for a while, but you and Mum just had to sit around, at home, wondering if I would live; and Mum was wondering, if I *did* live, whether I would be affected by the injuries to my head." Dad grinned at her. "Well, I came round, and I was all right, and Mum was so relieved that she brought you and Diane in as soon as the doctors said she could. Do you remember coming in to see me?"

Kate nodded. "Your head was covered in bandages, and your leg was hanging up in a big cage; and one of your arms was bandaged. In fact — " Kate grinned, too, "the only part of you we could see properly was your face, and *that* was cut and scratched."

"I was a bit of a sight, wasn't I?"

"I could hardly realise it *was* you," Kate admitted.

"Well, you see," Dad continued, "Mum just didn't know that you would be so badly affected. Do you remember having nightmares?"

Kate frowned. "I don't *think* so . . . it all seems a long time ago now . . . like a bad dream."

"That's just it," Dad continued, leaning forward. "It was a very bad dream for you, and you became nervous. You saw what a mess I was in, just with another car crashing into mine, and Mum began to have trouble with you crossing the road and other things. You used to scream at night . . . don't you remember?"

Kate shook her head. "Not really," she admitted. "It's strange, isn't it, because it's not very long ago. It seems to have been almost blocked out of my memory. I just know it was a horrible time. I remember you coming home, though."

"Well, Mum spoke to the doctor about you," Dad continued. "And he suggested you should take up a sport: swimming or tennis, something like that. So, of course, we decided it was time we let you have those riding lessons you'd always wanted. And we thought it had worked." Dad stopped, and they looked at each other.

"But I'm not afraid of crossing the road," Kate contributed.

"I know – that's why we thought you had got over it."

Kate sighed. "So what can I do about it?" she asked.

"Well, now you know *why* you feel afraid, perhaps it won't be so bad. It's not you being stupid or feeble. It's just shock because of my accident, coming out as fear of riding. You think you might fall off and end up like me." Dad looked at her, his eyes serious. "It's quite natural to feel nervous of doing something like riding. Almost anything can be dangerous, Katie, but if riding is something you really want to do, and as long as you act sensibly when you ride, then you should enjoy it and be safe. You can never be sure that someone else isn't going to do something stupid – just as that other driver did when I had the accident." He leaned forward. "But you can't let fear stop you doing *any*thing."

He grinned at her. "As soon as my leg is strong enough," he added, "I'm going to get another car, and drive again." He got up stiffly from Kate's bed, rubbing his leg. "I'll stop my lecturing now," he said, smiling down at her. "But you think about it. If you really think that pony is dangerous, then don't ride it. But Janet doesn't think it is." He chuckled. "She said all it really needs is love!"

When Dad had gone, Kate sat for a while, thinking. She thought about the Orange Pony; about its legs and how they must be hurting. She got up and opened her bedroom door. Across the hall, Mum and Dad were still in the lounge, reading the papers.

"I think I'll do my homework this evening," Kate called. "I'll go and see the ponies after dinner."

*

The stables were quiet when Kate walked in through the gateway and across the cobbled yard. Smudge, the black and white stable cat, turned her head to gaze at Kate coolly from her green eyes, before continuing to stalk her prey. With the tip of her tail twitching, she crept through the long grass at the back of the tack room, her body tense and ready to spring. Some poor little vole was doomed, Kate thought sadly.

The clatter of hooves sounded from the end stable, and Darkie's head appeared at the opening, a wisp of hay hanging from the corner of his mouth. He whickered and tossed his black head, snorting into the March air. Kate hurried over, digging into her pocket with her free hand to find a piece of carrot. Food was definitely the way to gain Darkie's devotion.

"How's that cough then, Darkie?" Kate asked, giving him the carrot. Darkie crunched the offering happily, while Kate chatted to him companionably. Then, gradually, she became aware of being watched. She turned her head. From the door opening, two stables away, the Orange Pony was looking at her.

Leaving Darkie to return to his hay, Kate approached the other stable cautiously. She had always kept well away from the Orange Pony, assuming that Tania reacted as dramatically towards humans as she did when in close contact with her equine companions. However, just now, the dun pony was looking towards Kate eagerly, her small, black-tipped ears pricked. As she approached, Kate thought what a pretty head Tania had. Her long, wispy mane hung daintily around wide-set, large brown eyes, between which a small white star showed. Tania's eyes watched Kate's approach uncertainly.

"It's all right, Tania," Kate said softly, remembering what Janet had said about the pony. "Don't be afraid." She lifted her good arm carefully and stroked the pony's pale brown neck. Tania pushed her nose hesitantly against Kate's coat.

"Yes, I can find some for you, too," Kate chuckled, pulling a piece of carrot from her pocket. She was surprised how gently Tania took the titbit with her soft mouth.

The sound of footsteps made both of them turn their heads. Janet was striding purposefully across the yard from the tack room, carrying a bucket and a head-collar. She smiled at Kate warmly.

"Oh, Kate, I'm so glad you came, after all. How's the shoulder?"

"Pretty sore still," Kate admitted.

"Have you seen Tania's legs?" Janet asked, stopping beside Kate. Kate shook her head.

"Thank goodness they didn't need stitching," Janet said, pulling the bolt on the stable door. Kate followed her into the stable and Janet put the bucket down. She smoothed Tania's neck and talked to her, before slipping on the head-collar. Tania snorted suspiciously towards the bucket.

"It's all right, Tania. It might hurt just a little, but it's to make you better." Turning towards Kate, Janet asked, "Do you think you could just hold the head-collar with your right arm, Kate? Just in case she moves about when I bathe her legs. Don't worry," she added, seeing the doubt spring into Kate's eyes, "she's really quite good. It's just easier if she stays still."

Janet was right. Kate held the head-collar and managed to tickle Tania under the chin at the same time with her good hand, whilst talking gently to the pony. Tania flicked her ears backwards and forwards nervously, listening first to Kate and then to the sound of Janet as she worked on the torn legs. Carefully, Janet unwound the bandages which the vet had applied. Then, very gently, she bathed the legs, dipping pads of cotton wool into the warm salted water, and dabbing cautiously at the cuts. She talked quietly, sometimes to Tania, sometimes to Kate, while she worked.

"There's a good girl – some of the places are just surface scratches, but one or two are a little deeper – steady, now – not deep enough for stitches, though, thank goodness."

Kate remembered what Dad had said. "How do you think she got free?" she asked.

Janet stopped for a moment. Sitting back on her

heels, she looked up at Kate. "That's what I can't understand," she admitted. "I'm very glad, of course. But I can't see how Tania freed herself. From the amount of scratching, it looks as though the wire had become quite badly entangled around her legs – and we couldn't actually *find* any barbed wire! It's a bit of a mystery," she added, bending down to continue with her work.

By the time the three o'clock ride had returned, led by Sally, Janet's young assistant, Tania's legs were bathed, and again encased in clean bandages. Kate hung about in Tania's stable while the riders dismounted. To her amazement, Tania on her own seemed to be gentle and friendly. Why, then, was she such a daunting prospect to ride amongst the other ponies?

"Is Janet right?" Kate murmured, stroking the pony's pale brown nose thoughtfully. "Are you so frightened – just like me? What a hopeless pair we are!" Tania blew through her nose softly, and nudged Kate's right arm. "Silly girl," Kate laughed, lifting her arm again to stroke the pony's neck, "I do believe you're asking for more attention!"

Kate felt Tania's neck muscles tighten. The pony's head lifted sharply, and her small ears flicked back, pressing themselves against her head.

"It's all right, girlie," Kate reassured her, stroking the dun pony as Lancelot was led close by the stable door. Kate turned her back on the stable opening and concentrated on smoothing Tania's thickly coated neck, trying to ease the pony's obvious tension and fear. Besides, she had no desire to see Paula. Paula's words haunted her mind, making her hate herself; making her repeat to herself, over and over, why oh *why* do I have to be so stupidly frightened?

But it was not Paula's voice which called in, "Hello, Kate. How's your arm?"

Kate turned quickly to see Clare peering in. Clare's fair-skinned face looked hot. She pulled off her riding hat with relief, and pushed her fingers through her fair, curly hair, which clung damply to her head where it had been pressed tightly under the hat.

"Phew! It's warm today. First day of spring, I think." Clare blinked and peered again into the stable, as if she could hardly believe what she saw. "What*ever* are you doing in with the Orange Pony!" she exclaimed. "I would have thought you'd have wanted to stay well away, after yesterday. *I* think Janet ought to sell her," she confided. "She's impossible to ride, as far as I can see."

A protective feeling swept over Kate. "Oh, no," she replied quickly. "She isn't – really."

Clare grinned. "Well, you could've fooled me!" she exclaimed, adding, "I think you're brave to have anything to do with her after yesterday."

"Paula thinks I'm stupid and —"

"Oh, Paula," Clare broke in contemptuously. "She's horrible."

"But I thought you were friends."

"No, we're not," Clare said, emphatically. "I don't know why you thought that. I'm glad she's gone."

"Gone?"

Lancelot shuffled impatiently at Clare's side. "I'll tell you in the tack room," Clare called, as she moved away.

Chapter 4

Kate liked the tack room. She liked the dim cosiness of its interior, and the smell of leather and ponies, combined with the clean, sharp smell of saddle soap. It looked particularly inviting that afternoon, with thin March sunshine shining in dusty shafts through the windows. A box of dusters sat on the old table, its contents straggling untidily across the table top.

"What needs cleaning?" Kate asked Janet, who hovered over the stable diary, checking riders and mounts for the next ride. Janet looked up. "Can you manage it, Kate, with one arm?" she queried. Kate nodded. "Well, make a start on Darkie's bridle, can you? He won't be needing it for a few days, so if you find you can't manage very well, you can leave it."

Kate found herself a bucket of warm water and a sponge, and lifted Darkie's bridle from its hook. She joined Clare on the bench next to the window. The tack room felt much more comfortable without Paula. Helen, a girl slightly older than Kate and Clare, also sat on the bench, busily rubbing at a snaffle bit.

Kate began to undo the straps with her right hand, using her left hand, gingerly, to hold the bridle.

"Where's Paula, then?" Kate asked Clare. Clare glanced towards Janet's desk before replying, but Janet was hurrying out into the yard, pulling on her riding hat as she went.

"She's gone!" Clare announced dramatically.

"But why?" Kate queried.

"Because of you, really, I suppose."

"Me?" Kate felt the colour rush to her face. "But I didn't — "

"Not *because* of you, exactly," Clare broke in, hurriedly, "but Janet was annoyed at the way she

was riding. It was Paula's fault that you fell off."

"It's been building up with Janet for a while," Helen put in. "She didn't like the way Paula rode. She *cares* about the way her ponies are treated. She was always telling Paula to stop yanking on Lancelot's mouth and not to shout at him."

"I didn't notice," said Kate.

"Well, you always keep in the background, don't you?" Clare pointed out.

Kate looked down at the ground. "Paula was always so — "

"Spiteful." Clare provided the word for her. "Yes. And I'm *glad* she's gone," she repeated. She grinned at Kate. "You should have been here this morning," she said.

"Why, what happened?"

"Well, you see," Clare began, "yesterday, when Janet came back from taking you home, she called Paula into the tack room."

"She looked – sort of – *severe*," Helen contributed.

"We knew something was up," Clare said. "You know how cheerful and friendly Janet is usually." She grinned at Helen, and then turned back towards Kate. "We hovered around near the stable door – we were cleaning out Charlie's stable, you see."

"And Janet was giving Paula a real ticking off,"

Helen continued. "She didn't exactly shout, but she sounded angry."

"And then Paula came stomping out of the tack room," Clare said, taking up the story, "looking very red in the face. And she rode off on her bike as if she couldn't get away fast enough!"

"And *then*, this morning, her mother came," Helen said. "She began to get shirty with Janet."

"But Janet wasn't having it," Clare put in, gleefully, her freckled face flushed with excitement. "She stood there, in the middle of the yard, and told Mrs Holt — "

"Janet looked really annoyed," Helen observed.

"She told her", Clare continued, "that her daughter had a lot to learn about the right way to treat ponies, and that she wasn't going to learn on Janet's ponies unless she did as she was told. She said that she had warned Paula several times, and that yesterday she was the cause of an accident because of her rough and ill-mannered riding, and that Mrs Holt should be thankful that nothing more serious had happened, as otherwise Janet would have held her responsible."

Clare had to stop for she had run out of breath.

Bewildered, Kate looked from one to another. She had hardly talked to these two girls before today. Somehow, Paula had always been there, looking at her disdainfully, and Kate had kept to herself, assuming that the three were good friends and that she must be an unwanted outsider. Now, however, it seemed that Clare and Helen were delighted to see the back of Paula!

"I didn't mean to cause any trouble," Kate began falteringly. "Paula will hate me even more now."

"I shouldn't lose any sleep over it," Helen advised. "She really needed taking down a peg or two, and Janet did it, that's all."

Clare beamed at Kate. "*I* don't mind," she said. "Now I can ride Lancelot. I like riding him best of all," she admitted, "and Janet used to book me in with him. But Paula wanted to ride him, too, and she used to keep on about it so much that I usually gave in."

The three girls settled down to their tack cleaning in companionable silence. Smudge, tired from her hunting, wandered in through the tack-room door. Leaping lightly on to the bench, she sat between Kate and Clare, washing herself delicately, her pink tongue carefully licking the short, black fur. Then, with a yawn, she curled up against Kate and slept.

Kate heaved a sigh of pleasure. The weekend had begun so badly, but now, despite an aching shoulder, she felt happy. She had two new friends, and out in the stable was the Orange Pony . . . She wondered why she felt differently about the

Orange Pony now. In fact, she was beginning to feel differently about riding, as well, since she had confided in Dad – and since the fall, too. Perhaps Dad was right and she could learn to not feel afraid, now she knew *why*. And maybe Janet was right about the Orange Pony – that she, too, was frightened. Kate wondered what had frightened *her*. Kate sighed again. It was all very puzzling.

Helen looked up. "Kate – you sound as though you've got the cares of the world on your shoulders!" she said.

"Oh no," Kate replied happily. "Quite the opposite!"

Chapter 5

It was one thing deciding that she felt better about
riding, Kate thought shakily, as she led Tania out of
the stable. However, it was quite another matter,
actually *doing* it. Already, Kate could feel the
tension in the Orange Pony, as they neared the
group of ponies in the yard.

Kate stopped. "There, that will do," she said,
trying to sound soothing, as she smoothed Tania's
tense neck. "I'll get on here."

Her knees were shaking as she lifted the saddle
flap to check the girth. But I must stay calm, she
told herself firmly, or else how can I help Tania to
feel more secure? She paused to fondle the dun
pony again, stroking her soft nose and talking to
her gently. Tania responded by pushing hopefully
into Kate's pocket.

"You're such a nice, gentle pony, you know,"
Kate told her, "when you can forget that you're
afraid. Come on," she whispered, gathering up the
reins in her left hand and preparing to mount, "let's
show them we're not really frightened!"

It was two weeks since either Kate or Tania had
been out for a ride. During that time, whilst Kate's

shoulder had been getting better, and Tania's legs were healing, Kate had spent as much time as possible with the Orange Pony. Each evening she had thrown her school bag on to her bed, changed quickly into old jeans and sweater, and called to her father, "Just going up to the stables, Dad. Won't be long. Back before dark. Is that OK?"

After a few evenings, Tania was waiting, watching, with pricked ears. As soon as she saw Kate, she would push her nose in the air and whinny, loud and strong. Darkie would pop his little head over his stable door, too, to whicker gently, before turning back to his hay. Pausing first to speak to both the ponies, Kate would then make her way to the tack room to fetch a bucket of warm water, into which she tipped some salt. Then, taking the packet of cotton wool from Janet's desk, she walked across the yard to Tania's stable. Janet had entrusted her with the evening care of Tania's injured legs, watching the nervous pony and nervous girl together with a secret smile.

As Kate worked, carefully bathing the scratched and torn legs, she talked to the dun pony, non-stop. Tania stood, her head down and turned slightly and her small ears flicking back to listen to Kate. Then, when she finished, Kate put the bucket in the corner. Opening the stable door, she led the pony out into the yard.

"We must keep her exercised a little, so that those legs don't get stiff," Janet had said, and so

together Kate and Tania walked round the small practice field, while Kate talked and Tania listened. When Janet came back with the evening ride, Kate knew that it was five o'clock and time to put the Orange Pony back in her stable. Janet let Kate give Tania her last feed of the day, and then it was time for Kate to say goodbye to both her favourite ponies.

Last weekend, Kate had spent all her spare time with Tania, and now she was going to ride her for the first time since her fall.

"Are all of you ready, then?" Janet called, scanning the group of assorted ponies and riders from Charlie's broad back. Charlie was sixteen hands – big boned, powerful and with a gentle, easy-going disposition. He gazed benignly about him as he stood, head and shoulders above the other ponies. Janet had built her riding stables from her two ponies – Charlie, the big powerful bay, and little Darkie, who had been her first childhood pony.

Kate, mounted now on Tania, hung back, away from the group of ponies. Clare, astride Lancelot, moved away from the others.

"How does she feel?" she called from a safe distance. Over the past two weeks, Clare, too, had been trying to help Tania by bringing Lancelot to the stable door. The grey pony had poked his head in through the opening and Kate had brought

Tania over, letting the two ponies sniff at each other cautiously.

Now, Kate felt Tania stiffen, and she stroked the pony's neck reassuringly.

"It's all right, girlie – it's just your friend, Lancelot," she told the dun pony. Then, to Clare, she replied, "OK, so far."

Lancelot stretched out his nose and snorted in Tania's direction. Kate held the reins gently but firmly, and talked to Tania. The dun pony's ears flicked back to listen, but she did not lay them flat against her head as she had always done before. Tentatively, she sniffed at the grey pony, her nostrils distended suspiciously. She squealed as Lancelot blew noisily at her, and Clare laughed.

"That's much more hopeful," she said. "More friendly than a pair of sharp heels or a nip on the shoulder!"

An hour later, as the evening ride made its way back to Oakhouse Stables, Kate felt a glow of satisfaction inside her which she had not felt before. As always, in order to avoid trouble, she and Tania were at the back of the straggling group of ponies. Kate looked at the dun pony's dark mane, which fell untidily on either side of her pale brown neck, and beyond to the small, delicately pointed ears, which constantly flicked back to listen to Kate's voice.

"You've been a *really* good girl," Kate told the flicking ears, and Tania pushed her head down and snorted noisily, as if in reply.

Clare, a safe distance in front but within earshot, half turned in the saddle. "She even understands what you say, now," she laughed. "She's *almost* a reformed character!" But, seeing Tania's ears flatten against her head as Lancelot's slower pace brought his hindquarters nearer, Clare urged her mount into a jog. "I don't think *I* want to ride her just yet, though," she added.

Watching Lancelot's ample rump jogging away, Kate was content. Life wasn't perfect. Tania was still frightened of her equine companions and Kate still feared riding, but neither of them was as frightened as they had been. And that must be a start, Kate reminded herself. Things could get better if she worked at it, she was sure. But the main reason for the glow of happiness inside Kate was the bond which had grown between herself and Tania over the past two weeks. Starting as a bond born of mutual fear, now it was a real bond of trust between horse and rider – a feeling which Kate had not experienced before. She suspected that it was a new feeling for Tania, too. The way to Darkie's heart had always been through Kate's bulging anorak pockets, for Darkie was, and always would be, Janet Delwood's pony.

Janet did not ride the little black pony now, of course, but a relationship, built up over many years, was obvious to the watchful observer. Janet would never pass by Darkie without giving the little black pony a pat or a few words, or a tickle behind the ears, and Darkie always knew the step that was Janet's. Only last month, a young rider had dismounted close to the water trough and had turned her back on Darkie to chat, thinking that he was drinking. A minute later, a shriek of surprise followed by much laughter had caused the chatting rider to turn round. Darkie had disappeared from beside her and only his back end could be seen, sticking out from the tack-room door! He had mounted the two wooden steps in search of Janet and, as Janet explained later, stood in the doorway, grinning at her!

As Kate brushed Tania down in the stable at the end of the day, she thought about the two ponies. She was very fond of Darkie; but old Darkie, friendly and obliging as he was, would always be Janet's pony. Tania was different. Tania was young and very nervous . . . and needed to be loved.

"Oh Tania," sighed Kate, flinging her arms around the dun pony's neck, "I *wish* you could be mine!"

But that could never be, Kate reminded herself, as the pony pushed a soft muzzle against her arm.

Mum and Dad could not afford luxuries like ponies. Life was difficult enough as it was, with Dad not at work. Besides, a city flat with a window box instead of a garden was hardly the place for keeping a pony!

"But I can still love you, can't I?" Kate whispered into one small, brown ear, and Tania snorted her approval.

Chapter 6

The Mystery, which had begun with Tania's injured legs, deepened on the following Saturday.

Tania was back again in the field with the other ponies, having been stabled for a few weeks while her legs healed.

On the Saturday morning, well before the first ride at nine o'clock, Kate and Clare walked down the hedge-lined path which led to the field where the ponies were kept. Although it was still early in the day, the spring morning was well under way. Spring flowers sparkled in the banks, the sky was blue, and birds darted everywhere, collecting nest material.

Kate hummed to herself. "Gorgeous, isn't it?" she said, happily, swinging the head-collar on her shoulder.

"Great!" Clare agreed. Then she pointed towards the field ahead.

"Look!" she said. "Tania's waiting for us at the gate."

"She doesn't seem to have seen us, though, does she?" Kate observed. "She's looking the other way."

Tania was looking down the lane in the opposite direction, her head up and her ears pricked. She heard the two girls' steps, as they drew nearer, and turned her head, whinnying a greeting.

"She really knows you now," Clare said, when they reached the gate and Tania pushed her nose against Kate's arm.

Kate laughed. "I think this could have something to do with it," she said, producing a piece of carrot from her pocket. She slipped the head-collar over Tania's soft muzzle and buckled the strap.

"That's funny," she mused gazing at Tania, a puzzled expression on her face.

Clare, just on her way across the field towards Lancelot, who was cropping the grass in a far corner, turned back.

"What is?" she asked.

"Well . . . it's just that . . . Tania looks as if she's been ridden."

"What, this morning?"

"Mm."

Clare came back to investigate. "I see what you mean," she said, smoothing Tania's dun back. "She's quite warm and sweaty – and look! The hairs from her winter coat that she's shedding – they're all pushed to the back of where someone would have sat, bare-back!"

"And look here," added Kate, moving Tania's long forelock to reveal a faint mark where a headband had pressed down the dun hairs. "She's been wearing a bridle!"

"So that's why she was at the gate!"

"And why she was looking the other way," Kate added.

The two girls looked at each other. "I wonder what Janet's going to say," Clare said, voicing the thoughts of both girls.

"She's not going to be very pleased," observed Kate.

"Oh well, I'll go and catch Lancelot and a couple of others, and then we'll get back to tell her."

Kate waited with Tania while Clare caught the other ponies. Then, when Clare was outside the field and the gate closed, Kate jumped up on to Tania's bare back and led the way down the path, back to the stables.

Because of Tania's behaviour in the company of other ponies, Kate could only bring the Orange Pony from the field, and had to keep her well away from the others. Clare rode Lancelot and led Saucy and Leo on either side. Secretly, Kate enjoyed this part of her day almost better than her official hour-long ride later on. Always, on the ride, she and Tania trailed at the back, keeping out of the way, but now they jogged ahead. Kate loved the feel of Tania's warm back, and she held the rope non-chalantly, pretending that she was a cowboy, riding her trusty steed across the plains . . .

"Hey, wait for me!" came a plaintive cry, disturbing Kate's daydreams, and reminding her that Clare had three ponies in head-collars to contend with.

"Whoa, girlie," Kate said, reining in her trusty steed. She was pleased to find that Tania responded, even though it was only to the pressure of a pulled lead-rope on the head-collar. "Good girl," she said, patting Tania's neck and enjoying again the feeling of a bond between them as Tania flicked one ear back and snorted. Turning, Kate watched Clare's progress with amusement. On one side of Lancelot, Saucy had decided that the grass was the best she had ever seen, and with her head down she was tearing at it as if she had not eaten all winter. On the other side, Leo had taken fright at a blackbird which had flown out suddenly from the undergrowth. Rooted to the spot, his head up and his nostrils distended, he was convinced that this dangerous creature was just a foretaste of terrible things to come, and refused to be moved. Between them, Lancelot stood patiently, while a not-so-patient Clare tugged at the lead-ropes.

"I can't budge either of them," Clare panted. She paused, looking towards Kate for inspiration.

"We-ell," said Kate, after some consideration, "I'm not sure I should suggest it, really . . . but perhaps if I just back Tania a bit, maybe . . . "

Squeezing with her heels and pulling on the

lead-rope, Kate persuaded Tania to back a few steps. Saucy, seeing the dreaded hindquarters advancing, raised her head sharply from the temptation of spring grass. Leo's attention, too, was diverted from one potential danger to another, and Clare was able to regain control.

"Thanks," she said, as they continued their way down the track.

"Did you notice", Kate called, turning round, "she didn't look quite as menacing as usual? She was too busy trying to do what I asked her."

For the rest of the jog down the lane, Kate's spirits were high. The Orange Pony, she told

herself, was marvellous to ride – when she could forget to be afraid of the other ponies. She could not imagine how she had not wanted to ride her. What Kate, herself, did not realise was that almost the same thing could be said about *her*. While she concentrated on encouraging Tania not to be afraid, she too was beginning to enjoy her riding. The whole look of her, astride Tania, had improved. Instead of hunching forward, round-shouldered, with her head tilted forward nervously and her hands high, clutching at the pony's mane, she sat straight and erect, looking much more comfortable and relaxed.

Janet noticed the change as they entered the small yard of the stables. She smiled at Kate.

"Tania's looking a lot happier," she remarked, "and I think it's all due to you, Kate. I think you're feeling better, too, aren't you?"

Kate nodded. She opened her mouth and was about to tell Janet of Tania's suspected early-morning rider, when Janet's attention was diverted by a call from the tack-room door.

"I can't find Tania's bridle *any*where!" It was Helen's exasperated voice which floated across the yard. She stood in the doorway, carrying an old rag and an opened tin of saddle soap and with a polishing duster over her shoulder.

"Are you sure?" Janet questioned.

"*Quite* sure. We've looked everywhere."

Kate and Clare looked at each other. The plot thickened!

"Someone might have stolen it!" Clare blurted out, and in answer to Janet's surprised and questioning look, she explained, aided by Kate.

Janet still looked perplexed when the two girls had finished their story. "I don't understand it," she mused. "Someone must be pretty desperate to ride. Why doesn't he or she come and have an hour's ride just like the rest of you?" She frowned. "I suppose I ought to contact the police." Looking up and seeing two more riders for the nine o'clock ride arriving early, she added, "I'll think about it later. Better borrow Darkie's bridle for now, Helen – let it out a bit and it should be all right for Tania."

Kate led Tania to her stable to groom her. It was hard work, for the dun pony's thick winter coat was being shed at a fast rate, revealing her brighter summer coat beneath. As Kate brushed and brushed, the dandy brush filled with hairs and had to be rubbed clear against the stable wall.

Pausing for a rest, Kate viewed the pile of dun hairs on the stable floor. "That should keep a few birds busy for their nests," she observed to Helen, who had just arrived with the saddle and Darkie's bridle, which had been extended to the last hole on either side of the cheek pieces. As Kate settled the saddle comfortably on Tania's newly brushed back, and reached underneath for the girth, Helen fitted the bridle.

"That's fine," Helen remarked, "it fits beautifully now." She lowered her voice and spoke conspiratorially. "You know, *I* think it's Paula."

"What is?"

"Stealing the bridle. I think she's peeved, and she's trying to get her own back."

"Mm . . . " Kate fastened the second buckle on the girth and paused to think for a moment. "But surely," she said, slowly, "she would ride Lancelot, wouldn't she?"

"Yes – I hadn't thought of that," Helen admitted. "Still, I bet it's something to do with her," she added darkly, as she let herself out of the stable.

Kate pulled at the leather and eased the stirrup iron down, tugging it sharply and tucking the end of the leather into place. As she walked slowly round Tania, to do the same on the other side of the saddle, she, too, wondered if The Mystery was connected with Paula. For a moment, she felt some of her old desperate fear return as she remembered Paula's scorn. Then Tania, who seemed to sense her fear, pushed her soft nose gently against Kate's arm, and Kate's newly found happiness returned.

Chapter 7

"I feel so *stupid*! Janet's going to think I made it all up."

The three stalwart helpers, Kate, Helen and Clare, were sitting in the tack room. Helen, who had just spoken, was gazing somewhat resentfully towards Tania's bridle, which hung innocently in its usual place.

"Don't be silly," commented Clare. "We all saw that it was missing. It's just The Mystery continuing."

The three girls had come in from mucking out two of the stables to have their coffee in the tack room, and the first thing that all three had noticed was Tania's bridle hanging neatly on its peg.

"Perhaps we should clean it," Kate suggested.

"I'm not going to touch it," Helen said hastily. "It might vanish in my hands!"

"Hey! I wonder if whoever it is is still hanging about," Clare suggested.

The three looked around, nervously, and Clare peered out of the cobwebbed and mud-splattered window of the tack room.

"It might be pony rustlers," Helen pronounced dramatically. "They may be stealing the ponies at this very moment, and be about to drive away in their concealed lorry!"

Clare laughed. "You're letting your imagination run away with you," she said. "There's only little Darkie in the stables – all the others are out on the ride. And who'd want to rustle Darkie?"

Nevertheless, they all trooped out to Darkie's stable to make sure that he had not been abducted. Darkie was delighted to see them – and to receive their offerings of half a chocolate biscuit, a quarter of an apple and a piece of cheese and cucumber sandwich. Now in a giggling state of hilarity, the three girls crept around the stable buildings, leaping out at each other at every possible opportunity. When Janet returned at the end of the ride, she found all three of them in the tack room in a condition of helpless mirth.

"Whatever's the matter with you three?" she enquired.

Helen wiped the tears from her eyes. "You're not going to believe this," she giggled, "but Tania's bridle came back – all by itself!"

As Helen had predicted, it took the three girls quite a while to convince Janet that they were not taking part in an early April Fool's joke. At last, when she had been persuaded, Janet decided that the next morning she would go with the girls to fetch the ponies from their field.

"I want to see if I can catch this phantom rider and bridle-stealer," she said, grinning at the girls.

"You *still* don't believe us!" Helen exclaimed.

"Yes I do," Janet replied, adding with a smile, "but just watch out next Saturday – it's April the first, you know!"

"Well, what a cheek!"

Janet, accompanied by the three girls, had rounded a corner of the lane which led to the ponies' field. It was early in the morning and the sun, still low in the sky, cast long shadows across the dew-covered grass. The ponies were all quietly cropping the grass in one corner of the field – except Tania.

Cantering in a large circle, in a patch of sunlight which highlighted the orange-gold of Tania's emerging summer coat which gave her her unusual name, the Orange Pony was being ridden by a boy. He rode her bare-back with just a piece of rope, which was arranged ingeniously to form an un-bitted bridle.

The boy wore old faded and patched jeans and an old loose pale blue T-shirt. He had red curly hair, and his face wore an expression of intense concentration. As the four watchers advanced, it was obvious that the boy had not seen them. Then, as he urged Tania to change legs in order to canter in the other direction, he noticed them, and a look of horror came over his face.

"I think I must have a few words with that young man," Janet said grimly as she broke into a run, followed by the three girls. But the boy had already headed Tania towards the gate. Pulling her up just short of it, he leaped down from her back and slipped off the makeshift bridle. Quick as a flash he had vaulted the gate and was running, in long strides, down the lane away from his pursuers.

"It's no good," panted Janet, stopping by the gate out of breath, as the red-headed boy disappeared down the lane, "I can't keep up that pace for long."

Snorting excitedly, Tania had watched their approach, and now she whinnied a welcome.

"*Now* do you believe us?" Helen questioned Janet, patting Tania's warm neck.

"I certainly do," Janet replied. She looked thoughtful as she added, "I'll say one thing for him – he can ride. Even so — " She was interrupted by a call from across the field. An arm waved from the other side of the hedge, and a quavering voice cried, "Hello – can you come over?"

Looking at each other with mystified expressions, the four climbed the gate and hurried over to the old man. He stood in a garden on the other side of the hedge, leaning heavily on two sticks.

"Do you want some help?" Janet asked anxiously.

"No my dear, thank you," the old man replied, "I just wanted to tell 'e something." He shifted uncomfortably and moved the position of his sticks. "Could 'e all come inside a moment?" he asked. "I've been poorly these last few weeks, d'ye see, and I'm none too steady on the old pins."

He showed them a small gate in the hedge and led the way down the path of his tiny garden and in through French windows to a small, comfortably furnished room, crowded with furniture.

"I won't keep 'e long," the old man promised, settling himself carefully into an old armchair which seemed to accept him with familiar ease. "Sit yerselves down."

Janet and the three girls sat down, slightly bemused by the happenings so early in the day.

" 'Twere a few weeks ago, 'afore I were ill," the old man began. "I can't remember when exactly." He paused and smiled around at them. "Time be a peculiar thing, d'ye see, when 'e get to my age. Well now," he continued, "what were I a-sayin'? Ah, yes. I get up early in the mornings – allus have done, since I were a lad, an' you can't change the habits of a lifetime. An' lately, I've seen that boy – the red-headed one." He chuckled. "Can't mistake that colour hair, can ye? Well, at first, all he did was stand at the gate and watch the ponies. I could see he meant no harm. He loved 'em, I could see that. I

54

love horses, too, d'ye see." He pointed towards some photographs on the mantelpiece. "I used to be a mounted policeman," he told them proudly.

Gradually the story emerged, as the old man recounted the happenings of recent weeks. At first, the red-headed boy had simply patted the ponies. Then one morning he had climbed from the gate where he usually sat, on to Tania's back, and had sat there, smoothing her neck and talking to her. The next morning he had arrived with his rope-bridle and had ridden Tania round the field.

"I wondered if I should call out," said the old man, "tell him he shouldn't be ridin' other folk's ponies. But, d'ye know, he rides well, and – I enjoyed watching him."

But a morning of the following week was the time that the old man was keen for Janet to know about. "I don't know how that barbed wire got in the field," the old man said, frowning as he remembered. "Someone ought to have known better. I looked out as usual, to see the ponies, and there was your little dun one in a terrible lather. She had the barbed wire caught around her front legs, and she were terrified. I fetched my coat and found a pair o' pliers and I started out, even tho' I weren't feeling so well that morning. But, you know, I'm so slow these days and by that time the boy was there. He had seen it too. He walked over, slow-like, towards the little mare. I could see him talking to her. Then he reached her and he acted very slow – just as he should."

The old man continued, describing how the boy had carefully slipped his rope round Tania's neck and then, still moving carefully and slowly, he had moved his hands down her leg towards the barbed wire, talking to Tania all the time. The mare had trembled with fear, breaking out in a sweat, but she had remained still while the boy had gently pulled the barbed wire away from the torn legs.

"He'd managed it by the time I arrived," said the old man. "She was free, although her legs were torn and bleeding." The old man looked across at Janet. "And *his* hands, too – they were badly scratched and bleeding. He hadn't even noticed. The little pony was quieter – she'd even started to eat the grass – so I said to the boy, 'Now, come along 'a me, me lad, an' I'll bathe those hands. Then we'll see to the pony.' An' you see by the time I'd bandaged his hands, I were feelin' proper poorly meself, an' the boy stayed while I waited for the doctor to call." He spoke to Janet in confidential tones, "Nice lad he is, d'ye see, but there's some trouble at home. His dad's in prison. Insurance fraud, he said, but his father's appealing against it – says he didn't do it, an' it were a genuine fire." He stopped to shake his head, sadly. "Sounds a sorry business – they're short of money, an' the mother's trying to carry on the business while the solicitor fights the case. They've got the local MP involved, too."

He looked round at them all. "So, you see, by the time we'd seen to the lad – Tom's his name – and then seen to me, you must ha' found the pony and taken her away. The boy had to go back home to help his mum. Real pickle, ain't it all?"

Janet looked thoughtful. "Well, Mr er — "

"Cribbs is the name – Stanley Cribbs."

"Well, Mr Cribbs, I'm very much obliged to you for telling me all this," said Janet. "It seems I have a big thank you to say to you – and to young Tom. The vet guessed it was barbed wire. He said if she had fallen, Tania could have been a lot worse." She smiled at him. "You've cleared up a mystery for us. Now, I'm afraid I must rush, or I'll be late for the first ride . . . "

Chapter 8

The solving of The Mystery was the talk of Oakhouse Stables that day. As Kate brushed Tania down, she shuddered when she thought of what might have happened if the red-headed boy had not freed the dun pony. She felt Tania's legs where the hair had grown over. She could feel only a slight raising of the skin where the sharp spikes of the barbed wire had clung to the pony's legs, tearing at the skin.

A thump, as Tania's saddle was balanced hastily on the lower door of the stable, broke Kate's reverie and made Tania jump.

"Sorry, Tania," Clare said. Then to Kate, she called, "I brought Tania's saddle and bridle at the same time as Lancelot's. We'll have to hurry, Kate – it's nearly nine, and all those keen little nine o'clockers are arriving." Clare hitched Lancelot's saddle more comfortably over her arm as she peered in at Kate, her face pink and full of excitement. "Janet's just had a *marvellous* idea," she confided. "She says she might organise a long ride in the Easter holidays!"

*

"A whole day of riding," Kate said, dreamily, leaning back against the tack-room wall and letting her imagination run riot. "It sounds heaven!"

"And it won't be too expensive for us," Clare said excitedly, "Janet said it would be a sort of 'thank you' to her regulars for all the help we give. Some of the others will have to pay more."

A sudden squall had sent the three girls scurrying into the tack room, and there they were discussing the proposed ride while they ate their sandwiches.

"How much will it be?" asked the practical Helen.

"The same as for an hour, for us," Clare replied, "but we'll be out *all* day, from about ten o'clock till fivish, and we'll have to take a packed lunch – and macs, which Janet says we can roll up and tie at the back of the saddle."

The excitement which quickened Clare's words was shared by the other two girls. None of them had ever spent more than an hour in the saddle, and the routes which Janet chose for the hour-long rides were, of necessity, fairly similar. Usually, they rode up the hill and on to the Downs, where they could canter and practise riding exercises.

As the school term drew to a close, Kate's excitement increased. Somehow, with all the preparations for the forthcoming trek, The Mystery

– now solved – was completely forgotten. The school term ground to a halt, and at last Kate was on holiday.

It was Thursday, and rain poured relentlessly from a leaden grey sky. Kate peered anxiously out of the lounge window, watching umbrellas and Wellington boots hurry past.

"It'll be really *awful* if it's like this on Monday," Kate said gloomily. "The ride will be ruined."

"Katie, don't be such a pessimist!" Dad rejoined. "You know what the weather's like at this time of the year – it can change from one moment to the next."

Dad was right. Within minutes, the grey clouds had blown away, leaving sunshine, blue skies – and shopping to be done.

"I'll go," said Kate, cheerfully. Dad's leg was aching this morning – because of the weather, he said – so Kate took the purse and shopping list which Mum had left. Pulling on her anorak, she let herself out of the front door of the flat, to walk along a pavement shining with puddles.

As she waited at the crossing for the green sign to appear and the bleeps to begin, Kate tried to remember being afraid to cross the road, as Dad had told her. But it was no good; that traumatic time of her life – such a short time ago – seemed to have been purposely forgotten. Her mood changed with the capricious turnabout in the weather, and

Kate hummed happily. Her own fear of riding seemed to have almost disappeared, too, thanks to the Orange Pony's nervousness and need for love. Surely Tania was improving, Kate thought. She remembered the red-haired boy riding Tania in a figure of eight in the field. She had cantered collectedly and held her head well and had changed legs easily. That meant she'd had a good early training, Kate mused, so someone must have cared for her and loved her. Some traumatic happening in Tania's life must have upset her, Kate decided, but like Kate herself she *could* be encouraged to regain her confidence.

Deep in thought, Kate wandered towards the door of the supermarket. Then something vaguely familiar caught her eye, and she looked up. Hadn't that been someone with red hair, just entering the supermarket? Had it been the boy? Grabbing a wire basket, Kate rushed through the door. It was! He was half-way down the first aisle, pushing a trolley.

"Hey! Wait a minute! Tom!" Kate broke into a run as the boy turned and recognised her. But the red-haired boy was not waiting to chat! After a horrified look in Kate's direction, he turned and ran, complete with trolley. He disappeared round a corner at the end of the aisle, with Kate in hot pursuit.

"Sorry!" panted Kate, narrowly missing a young

mother pushing a loaded trolley with a brood of bored toddlers in tow. She reached the end of the aisle. The red-haired boy was making for the exit, propelling his trolley at great speed down the next aisle. She was going to lose him!

Kate put on another burst of speed just as an old lady wandered across the end of the aisle, completely blocking the way with her trolley.

Luckily Tom's reactions were quicker than those of Kate, who skidded to a halt, almost falling into his trolley. The old lady looked at them in mild surprise and then continued to shuffle on.

Kate grabbed the red-haired boy's arm, determined not to let him get away. "Don't run away," she panted, "please!"

The boy turned a hostile face towards her. "Leave me alone, can't you?" he muttered. "I didn't mean any harm, riding the pony."

"I know!" Kate put in, hurriedly. "Janet knows too – that's the owner of the stables. She's not cross. She wants to see you – to thank you!"

The boy's face relaxed a little, but his eyes were still wary. "*Thank* me?" he repeated incredulously. "For riding her pony when I shouldn't?"

"No, silly — "

"Excuse me," an irritated voice interrupted, "I want to get to the sugar."

They moved away. "Come on," said Kate, looking at the boy's long list, "let's do our shopping, and I can tell you."

Chapter 9

It took a lot of persuasion, over packets of cereal, biscuits and tins of beans, before Tom was convinced. At last Kate made him understand how thankful Janet was that he had been able to save Tania from more serious injury.

"Janet wants to see you," Kate explained, as they carried their bulging plastic bags out of the shop. "She says that she needs some extra help in the stables at the weekends – *proper* help. We all help a bit, you see, but mostly we like being there to see the ponies and to talk about them. Janet said", she continued, cautiously, for she could see a lot of pride in Tom's thin, freckled face, "that if you liked, you could have some riding lessons, instead of pay – if you wanted."

Kate waited anxiously for his reply. She knew how it felt to think that people were looking down on you, and she desperately wanted Tom not to feel that Janet was doing him a favour.

Kate need not have worried. Tom turned towards her, his face alight with pleasure. "That's great!" he said enthusiastically. He grinned at Kate. "I think this is my lucky day," he continued. "We heard today that Dad has won his appeal. He's coming out of prison with his name completely cleared!"

It seemed to have been a week of good news for fathers, Kate thought to herself, as she shivered in the cold grey morning of Monday. Dad had been signed off by the doctor, and his old firm had telephoned to see when he could come back.

"There's a new company car waiting for me," Dad had said delightedly. He had looked towards Kate. "It'll take me a while to get used to driving again, but I'll manage, won't I, Katie?" he had said, smiling at her.

Now, as Kate dressed quickly in jodhpurs and a warm sweater, her thoughts turned excitedly to the day ahead. At last, it really was the day of the long ride!

Kate arrived much too early at the stables, but Helen was there already, and Clare arrived only a few minutes later on her bicycle, pink-faced and excited. Janet, arriving with the keys to the tack room, laughed when she saw them all hovering expectantly in the yard.

"I've heard of the early bird that catches the worm," she chuckled, "I presume these early birds are going to catch the ponies!"

There were ten ponies to fetch from the field, so Janet accompanied the girls. Back at the stables, Janet stood by the corn bins, measuring out oats, bran, flaked maize and pony nuts into ten buckets which the three girls brought.

"Don't forget," Janet reminded them, "enough water so that it isn't too dry, but not so much that it's sloppy!" For ten minutes the girls were kept busy, adding water to the buckets, stirring with wooden spoons, and carrying the food to the ponies. At last, all that could be heard was a contented munching from each stable.

"Kettle's boiled!" Janet called from the tack room. "Time for coffee!"

At a quarter to ten everyone was mounted; girths and stirrup leathers were being adjusted, anoraks and macs tied at the back of saddles. The ponies were excited, too – they could feel that something different was happening.

"How are we doing?" Janet called, looking down on them all from Charlie's saddle. "Has everyone got their lunch and a coat?" No one seemed to be without these two essentials. "Right. Off we go then – to the country!"

As Kate lay in bed the next day, idly watching patches of sunlight flicker and dart about her ceiling, and enjoying the luxury of a lie-in, she wondered why she felt so flat and somehow deprived – as if something had been taken away from her. She sighed, thinking how silly it was to feel like that, when yesterday had been so marvellous – and so exciting in such an unexpected way.

Kate's mind wandered back to the previous morning. A shiver of excitement had passed through the small band of ponies and riders, as they had set off from the stables. At the back of the group, following the wide grey rump of Lancelot ridden by Clare, Kate was sure that she could feel anticipation tingling through the reins of Tania's bridle.

"You know it's something different, don't you, girlie?" Kate whispered to the black-tipped ears which danced in front of her, as Tania swung her head excitedly. The Orange Pony looked about her curiously, for already the group of ponies was taking a different route from usual. They clattered down quiet Monday morning roads; past green-roofed houses, behind whose doors washing machines churned busily. Everything about this spring morning seemed better and more interesting than usual to the excited riders and ponies. Daffodils sparkled, golden and cheerful, in the sunshine; sheets and towels flapped importantly from clothes lines. Saucy, the little dapple-grey pony, skipped flightily across the road at the sight of an empty crisp packet; and even little Darkie, usually so slow and plodding, had a spring in his step.

Skirting the edge of the Downs, the group of ponies jogged past the zoo, and through an avenue of elegant horse-chestnut trees. At the top of the slope, Janet held up her hand, stopping the ride. Turning round in the saddle, she called out, "We'll be crossing the Suspension Bridge in a moment. I'll pay for us all, so don't worry about that." She grinned. "And if anyone is afraid of heights, don't look down!"

Ten ponies, plus Janet's big Charlie, made quite a clatter as they walked, single-file, across the Suspension Bridge. Gazing through the suspension cables which held the bridge, Kate shivered with a mixture of excitement and fear, as she saw a tiny tug chugging its way up the wide river, hundreds of feet below. Cars, looking like toys, moved by the river along a thin ribbon of grey which Kate knew to be a wide road.

Then they were on the other side of the gorge. The city was behind them, basking in spring sunshine, and ahead lay the country and a whole day of riding. Soon, Janet led the ride through iron gates and into a huge park. They trotted sedately along the tree-lined drive and then, turning off, Janet led them across the park land, urging Charlie into a canter, followed by the ten excited ponies. On the other side of the park, Janet reined in Charlie and they all stopped by a small gate. The ponies snorted, excitedly.

"That was great!" enthused Clare, turning round to Kate, her round face pink and glowing.

Kate patted Tania's neck, enthusiastically, and the Orange Pony snorted and tossed her head. "It was the longest canter I've ever had," admitted Kate. "It was wonderful – just like flying!"

"Leo bucked at the beginning!" said Helen.

All around them, an excited chatter broke out. Janet's voice called above the hubbub, "Now listen a minute everyone! We'll be on the road again for a while, once we go through this gate. It's quite a busy road – cars drive very fast along it – so take care, please; single file and walking. It won't be for long. Soon we'll turn off down a track. Off we go, then!"

Once through the gate, the ponies kept to the grass verge at the side of the road, walking in single file. As Janet had said, cars whizzed by at great speed, and all the riders were glad when Janet held her riding crop out firmly to the right and led the file of ponies nearer to the centre of the road. When the road was clear, they crossed to a farm track, rutted and muddy, but free of traffic. Soon the road was out of sight and the young riders felt that, at last, they really were in the country.

On one side of the muddy track was a field of cows. Some young heifers trotted over to get a closer view of the visitors. They crowded together at a gate, pushing their noses between the bars and blowing noisily. Kate noticed their flat faces, and their wide-set, curious eyes with long lashes.

"They've got pretty faces," she called to Clare, who was leaning over, trying to smooth one of them.

"They're sweet, aren't they?" Clare replied. "I wonder what they'd be like to ride!"

Janet, who had overheard the conversation, laughed. "Pretty uncomfortable, I should think," she said. "I'd rather stick to Charlie!"

The boundary of the field ended at a hedge, and the heifers were left, standing disconsolately in the corner, watching them out of sight.

On the other side of the path, a tractor trundled its way across a partly ploughed field, followed by a noisy flock of seagulls.

"Makes you think you're at the seaside when you hear those noisy birds," Clare remarked, turning slightly in Lancelot's saddle to speak to Kate.

Kate nodded. "It's lovely here, isn't it?" she asked. "And such a gorgeous day. I don't want it to end." But, for Kate, the real excitement of the day had not even begun.

Chapter 10

A little further on the lane turned in to a large, untidy farmyard, where brown and white hens, squawking noisily, scuttled out of the way of the ponies.

"This is our headquarters for lunchtime," Janet called out. "Unsaddle your ponies now, and put on their head-collars. Let them have a drink, if they want one, over there – " she pointed in the direction of a water trough in one corner of the yard " – and then tie them up along that hedge." She swung her arm around in the direction of a gate leading to a field. "They can crop the grass and have a rest, while we have our packed lunches. You can prop the saddles against the hedge, but make sure they can't be trampled by any of the ponies."

Slipping her feet out of the stirrups, Janet slid from Charlie's saddle. "I don't know about you," she added, "but I'm starving! Ah – here comes Mrs Scammell!"

Mrs Scammell and her husband, who appeared later, were, as Janet explained, friends of Janet's family who were allowing Janet and her band to use the farmland for a couple of hours. She came out of the farm door bearing a large tray, which contained several jugs of homemade lemonade, paper mugs and two huge slabs of fruit cake.

"I don't think I've *ever* been so hungry!" exclaimed Clare, when the ponies had been safely secured by the hedge and the girls had thrown themselves down in the shade. However, packed lunch followed by Mrs Scammell's fruit cake and lemonade, soon overcame this problem.

"Gosh, I'm full!" exclaimed Helen, stretching full length under the hedge.

Kate laughed. "There's no pleasing you two!" she said.

"It's hot," murmured Clare sleepily, leaning against the hedge and squinting at Lancelot through half-closed eyes.

"It's lovely," said Kate contentedly. Tania was at the end of the line of tethered ponies, and Kate could just see her apricot-coloured quarters and the bow of red ribbon at the top of her tail. "I wish we could do this every day," she murmured.

A couple of the riders wandered off to investigate the farmyard, but most of the others sat or lay in the shade. Closing her eyes, Kate listened. All she could hear was the steady tearing and munching of the ponies' teeth, the buzzing of insects and, in the distance, the slow rumbling noise of the tractor; apart from that – nothing – just the peaceful silence of the country.

"Come on you sleepy heads!" Janet's amused voice broke their reverie. Kate sat up quickly. "We're not going to waste our day out, snoozing under a hedge, you know," laughed Janet. "Here you are – one each."

She handed out a piece of paper to each rider. On each piece was a list.

"What's this" asked Helen, "A feather – sheep's wool – whatever – ?"

"It's a treasure hunt," Janet explained.

When the ponies had been saddled up and their riders had mounted, Janet spoke from Charlie's broad back.

"Now then," she said, looking at her watch, "I make it half past one – can you all put your watches to the same time?" She waited while they adjusted their watches, and then she continued. "You've all got your haversacks on, have you? – good. Well, I want you all back here at two o'clock, and the one with the most things from the list will win a prize! Don't leave any gates open, for goodness' sake, or Mr and Mrs Scammell won't let me bring you again." Janet paused to let her warning have an effect, and then she continued. "I'm trusting you to be sensible. Oh, and don't forget to check your girths before you set off – you'll be doing a lot of getting on and off." Everyone pulled up saddle flaps and checked the girths, some notching them up a hole. "Off you go!" Janet said at last, "and

74

enjoy yourselves. Back at two o'clock sharp, or else you'll be disqualified!"

Ponies and riders fanned out across the field. Kate and Clare both made for the farmyard, each deciding independently that she would try to find one of the hen's feathers.

Two brown feathers were found almost immediately, and tucked into the two haversacks.

"That makes a start, anyway," mused Clare, studying her list.

"There must be sheep somewhere," Kate said, "otherwise Janet wouldn't have sheep's wool on the list. I'm off to hunt for the sheep!"

"Good luck!" Clare called, as she headed back to the field. "I've seen some clover – I'm going to get that next."

Kate set off down the track which they had all ridden up earlier in the day. They had turned in at the farm entrance, but she had seen that the track continued. She felt sure that there would be sheep somewhere . . .

As Tania jogged down the track, Kate realised, with a sudden surge of delight, that this was the first time that she had ever ridden alone. It was a wonderful feeling – especially with the Orange Pony.

"You're lovely, Tania," she whispered, patting the pony's golden neck. "I wish we could ride like this for ever! Oh, I wish you were mine!"

Kate daydreamed, quite forgetting to look for sheep. The afternoon was quiet, with only the sound of Tania's thudding hooves, birdsong, and the buzzing of insects. Suddenly, she became aware of movement and noise to her right. Turning her head, she saw a chestnut pony careering across a field, its reins and stirrups flapping, and with no sign of a rider. Noting quickly that the pony was not one from Oakhouse Stables, Kate squeezed Tania into a fast trot. Soon she found a gate leading into the field. Dismounting, she opened the gate, led Tania through, closed the gate and mounted again.

"Now, let's see if we can find that pony," Kate murmured to the Orange Pony, forgetting all about the treasure hunt, "or perhaps its rider."

Urging Tania into a canter, Kate followed the direction of the chestnut pony's wild gallop. As they reached the brow of the hill, she saw the pony. It was cropping quietly in one corner of the field. Kate spoke quietly to Tania. "Steady, girlie," she said, "we mustn't frighten him."

They walked down the slope towards the other pony, which eyed them nervously, but continued to eat. It was a lovely pony, Kate decided, as they approached it, slowly. It had good proportions, with fine, clean legs and a beautiful small head, which it now raised, watching them warily. Slowly

Tania came closer to the chestnut, until Kate was able to lean over to pick up the reins. It was only when the reins were firmly in her hand that Kate realised she had asked the Orange Pony to do something which, only a matter of weeks ago, she would have found impossible.

"*Good* girl," Kate murmured. "Now let's see if we can find the rider."

With new-found confidence, Kate led the chestnut pony and headed Tania back up the slope in the direction from which the chestnut had first come galloping.

The field was large. It narrowed at one end into a wide path, next to a copse. Holding on to her charge firmly, and speaking to Tania as they went, Kate followed the path until, suddenly, she heard a voice calling.

"Help!" it called. "I'm over here. Please help me!"

Kate could see someone huddled against the hedge. As the two ponies approached, Kate could see that it was a girl. Then —

"Kate! It's *you!*" The voice was disbelieving.

Kate stared down at the girl's tear-stained face and when she spoke, her voice, too, was disbelieving.

"Paula! Is that really you? Are you hurt?"

"Yes – I think I might have broken my leg. I can't

move it – it hurts too much."

"Well, don't worry," said Kate, "I'll soon get you some help. The farm isn't far away. I won't be long, I promise."

"But – but, can you manage. I mean – the Orange Pony – and you – " Paula's voice trailed away.

"Of course I can. Tania's really good now." Kate's confident voice belied her true feelings. In order to return to the farm, Kate would have to turn the two ponies round in a confined space. What would Tania think of that? Would she forget and kick out at the chestnut pony? Tania wasn't so *very* good – she still wore her red ribbon, and other riders still kept their mounts well out of her way.

Kate could not bear to think of Paula's scorn afterwards, if she messed it up now. She could imagine her, later on, leaning back with her leg in plaster, telling her friends, "She was just as hopeless as ever – that Orange Pony kicked out at mine, and Kate fell off – and she *cried* – "

Taking a deep breath, Kate leaned down and pushed at the chestnut pony's neck, at the same time squeezing Tania behind the girth with her left foot and turning her head towards the other pony. She felt Tania stiffen. This was just too much close contact, and Tania's ears flicked back. The chestnut pony sensed the tension and looked as though he would play up.

Summoning up her firmest voice, Kate said, "Come *on*, Tania, *behave* yourself. Round you go." She gave the chestnut pony an extra push with her right hand. "And *you* behave, too," she commanded. Kate was surprised to hear her own voice sounding almost cross!

Miraculously, the two ponies moved obediently, turning and walking off meekly down the path when Kate instructed them. Kate called over her shoulder, "I'll be as quick as I can!" to the huddled figure on the path. Inside her head, she sang triumphantly, "How about that, then, Paula Holt!"

"Might as well be killed for a sheep as a lamb," Kate muttered to herself, as they entered the field.

She squeezed firmly with her heels and Tania broke into a canter. The chestnut cantered alongside, held tightly by Kate, and in no time they had reached the gate. Kate slipped down from the saddle to open the gate. She kept the two ponies as far apart as possible, but held them firmly and spoke to them sharply if they began to look doubtful about their close proximity.

Despite her apparent confidence, Kate found that her knees were shaking violently as she opened the gate and led the two ponies through. She managed to re-mount without mishap and she trotted the ponies down the lane, turning in through the farm entrance to the yard, where Janet was standing, talking to Mrs Scammell.

"Kate!" Janet's face was amazed. "You're back on time – but I didn't have a pony on my list!"

"It's Paula Holt!"

"Paula?"

"Yes. She's hurt. She thinks she's broken her leg. She's in a field over there." Kate waved an arm in the direction of the field where she had left Paula. "It's not far." She looked towards Mrs Scammell. "I think we ought to send for an ambulance!"

"I'm afraid I messed up the treasure hunt for you," Kate said. Ponies and riders were standing, ready to move off on the homeward journey. The ambulance had been and gone, taking a pale-faced Paula with it, and the chestnut pony was temporarily housed in one of the many outbuildings at the farm until Paula's father, who had been contacted, could come to fetch him. Mrs Scammell had known where to telephone, for the Holt family had recently come to live close to the farm. Mrs Scammell told Kate that Paula had only just been given the chestnut pony.

"Nonsense, Kate," Janet replied warmly. "I think everyone enjoyed the excitement – and we shared the prize!" After all the excitement, Janet had opened the tin of sweets which had been the treasure hunt prize, and had had no difficulty in disposing of its contents amongst the riders.

"I think you all enjoyed yourselves, didn't you?" Janet asked the assembled group, and a murmur of assent rose from her charges.

"I would have been disqualified anyway," Helen pointed out cheerfully. "I was enjoying myself so much I forgot the time!"

"Well, before we go," Janet called out, "I have something important to do." Looking towards Kate, she continued, "You all know how Kate and Tania came to Paula's rescue. Well, when I saw Kate riding Tania and leading Paula's pony, I realised just how much they both have improved – Kate in her confidence and Tania in her behaviour towards other ponies." Janet smiled at Kate and reached over towards the Orange Pony's rump. "I think it is time that this" – she pulled at the bow of red ribbon – "should go!" With a flourish, Janet pulled the ribbon right off.

Chapter 11

Of course, that was it! As Kate lay in bed, thinking over the events of the previous day, she realised suddenly why she felt deprived – as if she had lost something. She was pleased, of course, that Tania would no longer wear the red ribbon. After all, that was what – with Clare's and Lancelot's help – she had been working towards. But, with the removal of the red ribbon, Kate felt almost as though she had lost that special bond between herself and Tania.

Back at the stables, after the day's ride, Kate had left Tania in her stable while she went to prepare the evening feed. When she had returned, she had been surprised to find two of the younger riders in the stable with the Orange Pony. They were patting her and stroking her nose.

"She's really pretty, isn't she?" Kim said, when Kate opened the stable door.

"I didn't know she was so gentle," said the other little girl, Rachel, gazing at Tania with adoring eyes. "I'm going to ask Miss Delwood if I can ride her next week!"

Some of the other riders, too, had stopped on their way past the stable door and had looked in at Tania. Kate could see that they were viewing the Orange Pony with different eyes, and Kate heard them discussing the possibility of riding Tania soon.

Kate sighed. She had to own up to the fact that she wanted to keep the Orange Pony to herself. She did not want to share her with the others.

"I'm being horrible," she told herself firmly. "If Tania is better behaved with the other ponies, then it means that she is not frightened any more. And *I* know what a lovely feeling that is." She sat up in bed and looked at her clock. "Goodness! Ten o'clock."

Splashing her face quickly with cold water, Kate dressed in her old clothes and went to the kitchen to grab some breakfast before making her way to the stables to see the Orange Pony.

On the table in the kitchen was a note which stopped her in her tracks.

"Oh no!" she moaned.

The note read, "Don't forget you are meeting me at Dickon's for lunch at 12.30 – shoes and Aunt Brenda. Love Mum."

Kate sat down dejectedly on her chair. She sighed. She *had* forgotten. What a nuisance shoes were – and aunts! She remembered now that Mum was taking a half-day off to buy her some new shoes – "Yours are falling to pieces, Katie," she had declared, looking in despair at Kate's down-at-heel footwear. "I don't know *what* you do with them!"

Then Mum had decided that, since they would be in the centre of the city, they might as well go to visit her sister. "I haven't seen Brenda for ages," she had said, "and I expect Jenny and Edward will be there."

Kate poured cereal into a dish and sighed again. Seeing Jenny and Edward was no real incentive, she decided. Jenny was all right, if a bit uninteresting since she did not like ponies – but Edward . . . Oh well, life was full of these little frustrations, Kate told herself, philosophically, finishing the cornflakes. She washed her dish and left it to drain. Then, with a slight air of martyrdom, she returned to her bedroom to change. Old jeans and a sweater with holes in the elbows were definitely not correct wear for today!

Just as Kate was pulling her respectable blue sweater over her head, the telephone rang.

"Probably Mum, making sure I'm awake," Kate thought, with a grin. But the voice on the other end of the telephone line was not instantly recognisable.

"Is that Kate?"

"Ye-es . . . "

"Kate, this is Myra Holt – Paula's mother."

"Oh – hello, Mrs Holt – er, how's Paula's leg?"

"Well, it's in plaster – it *was* broken, but a clean break, the doctor said, so all she has to do now is be patient and keep her leg up."

"Poor Paula," Kate murmured, thinking really of the beautiful chestnut pony, "she must be fed up, with the holidays here and not being able to ride."

"That's just it, Kate," Mrs Holt continued, "and she wondered if you would like to come over to see her, perhaps for the weekend – just for some company, you see, and maybe to ride her pony, if you would like that."

"Me? Ride Paula's pony?"

"I know he's a bit of a handful," Mrs Holt's voice sounded anxious, "and I'll telephone again, of course, to ask your parents, but", her voice lowered a little, and took on a confidential tone, "he's a very *good* pony, you see – we paid a lot of money for him – it's just that – well, Paula isn't very good with him, yet, and we thought that perhaps you . . . " She hesitated, and then continued, "Paula told us, you see, about how you seem to have calmed down that pony – the Orange Pony, isn't it? – and Paula seems to think that you might be able to help Firefly, too. We would be most grateful if you would . . . " Mrs Holt's voice trailed away, leaving Kate momentarily speechless on the other end of the line. She could not believe that she, Kate, who only two months ago had felt so desperately unhappy because of her fear of riding, was actually being asked to ride a difficult pony, with the hope that she could calm it down. In actual fact, she had no doubt that Firefly was not really a difficult pony at all, but was simply reacting to Paula's insensitive riding – it was probably Paula who needed the help, rather than Firefly!

As Kate arranged the visit to Paula's house for the following Friday, her heart sang. Suddenly, life seemed wonderful. She was no longer frightened of riding; Tania was at the stables waiting to be loved by Kate and ridden by her every week; suddenly there was another pony to be ridden, too – and maybe Paula wasn't so bad, after all.

Humming to herself, Kate tied up her worn shoes. Even the thought of having to visit Cousin Edward could not spoil her mood. Life was wonderful – and it was all thanks to the Orange Pony!